Up on the Housetop
-A Christmas Story-

by
Bradley McBride

© 2021 Bradley McBride

All rights reserved. No part of this book may be reproduced in any form or by any means without permission from the author, Bradley McBride.

Visit www.thuswesee.com

First Edition, November, 2021

Published by Addept Media, LLC, Gilbert, AZ

Library of Congress Control Number: 2021950494

ISBN: 978-0-9886223-5-7

Printed in the United States of America

Up on the Housetop

-A Christmas Story-

by
Bradley McBride

To my father and sons

FOREWARD

There are two Christmas stories that are ingrained in tradition and in my heart. One is *A Christmas Carol* by Charles Dickens. The other is *How the Grinch Stole Christmas* by Dr. Seuss. Both stories are about a Christmas-hating curmudgeon experiencing a change of heart. I love both of them.

These are deservedly classic stories that have not only endured but have been revisited time and again in film and television for generations. Why? Because we like seeing people change for the better. Both Ebenezer Scrooge and the Grinch experienced a change of heart specifically regarding Christmas. Reading about their evolutions makes us feel good and gives us hope that we too can change.

Here's my problem: In neither *The Grinch* nor *A Christmas Carol* is there any reference to the very reason Christmas exists in the first place: Jesus Christ. He is not mentioned in either, and barely alluded to in the Dicken's classic. Not quite secular, but close. Scrooge's change of heart came about because spirits visited him and showed him how messed up he was. The Grinch's heart grew two sizes that day because the people of Whoville gathered to celebrate Christmas without the commercialization.

Neither experienced the "mighty change of heart" that comes from the Atonement of Jesus Christ, through the Holy Spirit.

I've thought about that for a long time. How does one learn to love the true meaning of Christmas while essentially ignoring the Savior and His role in changing hearts?

This story is my attempt to bring Jesus into a modern story of how hearts can change, especially at Christmastime. Be forewarned: It isn't a fluffy Christmas story. Hopefully, it will cause us to dig a little deeper when we think about personal Christmas miracles.

Merry Christmas!

Brad

Up on the Housetop
- A Christmas Story -

11:50 p.m.

I pronounced it as clearly as I could: "Hey, Com-pooo-ter, turn on the Christmas tree." The digitized woman's voice emerged from the little box on the mantel above the fireplace. "Now playing 'O Christmas Tree,' from the playlist Christmas." The music filled the room.

"Hey, Com-pooo-ter, stop the music." The music didn't stop. I tried again, but louder: "Hey, Com-pooo-ter, stop the music!" This time it stopped.

I muttered to myself, "Yeah, right. Pretty dumb for an 'Artificial Intelligence.'"

My wife, Amie, who was sitting cross-legged on the floor near the Christmas tree, put down the package she was wrapping and looked at me with an equal degree of frustration. Pointing her scissors at me, she said, "Maybe if you would just pronounce 'Computer' correctly, it would understand."

"I'm trying to teach it to respond to 'Com-pooo-ter,' because that's the way Gracie says it."

"Yeah, but Gracie's three. She'll grow out of it before you're done there."

"Maybe so. But it's sure cute now."

"True. But Sam, you've been messing with that stuff for hours, and I really need some help. Please?"

"It's complicated!" I protested. "I have the thermostat, the outside lights, and the stereo all hooked up now. This is the last thing, and then I can help wrap presents."

I heard Amie say softly, "By then I'll be finished."

It would have been smart to just stop, but I just had to get the last word in. That little voice in my head told me to bite my tongue, but I ignored it. "You know, Amie, you've been buying gifts since Halloween. You didn't have to wait until Christmas Eve to wrap them."

I instantly regretted it. Amie stopped and glared at me. "We don't all hate Christmas like you do. Can you cut me some slack?"

"I . . . I . . . don't hate Christmas per se." Whenever you inject 'per se' into an argument, you know you are losing the argument. "I get so exhausted about the run-up the months before, and it's just all the commercialization and the hassle—I think it kills the Christmas spirit." It sounded disingenuous even as it came out of my mouth.

"Oh, so now you're suddenly worried about the Christmas spirit? Fabulous."

"No, really! I hate the expense, and the stores, and the shopping, and the expense. And the stress," I said.

"You said 'expense' twice, and I can tell where this is going."

"Well, my favorite part of Christmas is the . . ."

She interrupted me with a mocking tone, ". . . the day after Christmas, because then we can just relax, yada, yada, yada. You say the same thing every year."

"I mean it every year!"

She didn't respond.

There is an old saying: *If you find yourself in a hole, stop digging.* I've never quite mastered that. I kept digging.

"So how much is Christmas costing us this year? You know the renovation is killing us."

"I stayed within the budget that you agreed to."

"Whoa. Christmas miracle?"

She looked at me with exasperation. "I don't get it. Do you sit around at work and think up hateful things to say to me? You seem to be getting better at it all the time. You can be such a . . ."

And she stopped.

"A what?" I prodded.

The tension in the room was equaled by the silence. I stared at the A.I. instructions on my phone as she pushed the last package under the tree, stood up, and said, "I'm finished and I'm going to bed."

Before she left the room, Amie put her hands on the back of the couch. With a voice tinged with sadness, she said, "Will you at least go upstairs and check on the girls?"

"Yeah."

She said one last thing, gently, sincerely: "Look, I know you have Christmas issues because of your dad, but you're a dad now. Somehow you need to get past this. For eleven months out of the year you are wonderful, but I can't live like this every Decemb . . ."

She stopped, dropped her head without finishing her thought, and continued down the hall to our bedroom.

As she walked away, I thought heard a sniffle. No, I'm sure I heard a sniffle, but chose to ignore it. Had I known what was coming, I would have chased after her and tried to fix things. I didn't, so I didn't.

12:20 a.m.

I had been staring at my phone like it was the most important thing on earth, but I wasn't seeing it. I sighed and mentally chastised myself. The stereo was softly playing some classic Christmas carol from a streaming playlist someone had created. I fiddled around with the settings for a few more minutes, then finally set my phone down next to the A.I. box and headed up the stairs to the girls' room. I could fix the computer the next day. I doubted anyone except me would care anyway. There would be plenty of time to mess with it when Gracie and Sarah fell back asleep after checking out their presents from Santa. After that, we could proclaim Christmas officially over and done with for another year.

We had a narrow, decorative table at the top of the stairs. We put our Nativity set there, one of the "too many" Christmas decorations we had already amassed in ten years of marriage. This Nativity, however, was a beautiful thing that we'd bought while travelling in Europe. It was made of wood, hand-carved with intricate details. As I walked past, I noticed that the baby Jesus piece was missing from the manger. Again. I knew right where it would be. From the moment Amie took it out of the box and set it up, Gracie felt compelled to carry the baby Jesus around with her. The carved infant was about the size of a walnut. We tried to get her to leave it be, but she was a sneaky one.

I went into the girls' room, which was gently lit by the tiny Christmas tree Amie had set up on their dresser. Gracie had already kicked off her covers, so I went over to tuck her back in and give her a kiss.

As I stepped next to the bed, I found the baby Jesus—right under my foot. I jumped and held back a yelp. When I reached down to pick it up, I noticed that the angel from the Nativity set was on the floor next to it. I quickly checked them out and was glad to find that I hadn't broken anything. I tucked them both in the pocket of my sweatpants until I could put them back where they belong.

I pulled the covers up over Gracie's little body and tucked them under the mattress to stay put. I leaned and gave her a kiss on her cute forehead. She was out cold.

"Hi, Daddy." Sarah had been watching me from across the room.

"Hey, Punkin, you're still awake? Too excited to sleep?"

"I'm sorry. I promise I've been trying! But tomorrow's Christmas!"

I could hear the sincerity in her voice. I glanced at my watch. "Actually, today is Christmas—it is after midnight already."

"Do you think Santa came?" Five years old is peak

age for Santa fascination.

"Nah, I was just downstairs, and he hasn't been here yet. But I'll bet he'll be here soon. You'd better get to sleep."

"I hope he can find us in our new-old house."

I chuckled at her use of "new-old house." It was true. The house was new to us, but it was a very old house. One hundred seventy years old, give or take. And, as it turns out, every single part of it needed to be fixed or replaced. Who can afford Christmas?

"Oh, don't worry about Santa, sweetie. He'll find you. He has magic, you know. Now keep trying to go to sleep, and Christmas morning will be here before you know it. Give me a kiss."

Sarah sat bolt upright at the exact second I bent down to kiss her. The crown of her head slammed into my nose, and I thought I heard a crunch.

"Dang it, Sarah! How many times have I told you to not do that?"

"I'm sorry, Daddy. It was an accident." Sarah started to cry.

I consoled her and told her all the right things, but I did it quickly because I could feel my nose starting to bleed. I think she finished crying before I left the room, but I'm not positive.

"Congratulations, Sam," I said to myself, "Christmas Eve and you already have half of your family in tears. Nice going."

I grabbed some tissues out of the girls' bathroom and headed back downstairs. Yes, it was bleeding, but as I felt around it, nothing moved that probably shouldn't. I pinched the bridge of my nose and tilted my head back so the blood would stop. I probably needed some ice.

When I came back down the stairs to the family room, I saw the A.I. box and gave it one last shot:

"Hey, Com-pooo-ter. Enter bedtime mode."

The gentle voice replied, "Entering bedtime mode. Goodnight." The music turned off. The Christmas tree lights turned off. Even the outdoor lights turned off. Hah! I actually did it! So cool! I debated about getting ice for my nose and decided just to clean up and go to bed.

I was feeling pretty good about myself for a moment, until I entered the bedroom and remembered that I shouldn't be feeling too good about myself. Amie was already in bed, covers up, facing the wall away from me. I stood next to the bed, looking at her back. I knew I needed to say something.

"Hey, Honey..."

Nothing.

"Amie?"

I realized that she had already put in her earplugs, or what she referred to as her "anti-Sam snoring devices." It kinda felt like she was still awake, and the little voice in my head told me to wake her up and apologize, but I decided not to push it. Besides, if she wanted to talk, she would have waited up for me, right? She was obviously not in a talking mood. That was okay, because neither was I. This type of scenario played itself out more and more frequently as of late.

I closed the bathroom door before I turned on the light. I was surprised that my nose and face weren't bloodier. The bleeding had already stopped. Maybe I'd overreacted a little. I washed my face and brushed my teeth, took off my watch, turned out the light, and went back into the bedroom.

Quietly, I took off my sweatpants and t-shirt and draped them over a chair, then slid into bed, careful to make as little motion as possible. If Amie was asleep, then I sure didn't want to wake her and start a discussion. If she was already awake, well, then she must not want a discussion.

1:45 a.m.

Sleep didn't come easy. In fact, it didn't come at all. I lay on my back, staring at the dark ceiling, listening to Amie's steady breathing, which let me know that she was definitely asleep. Normally, the quiet security of the sound of her breathing helped lull me to sleep. Tonight was different. I could tell sleep wasn't coming. I wasn't looking forward to Christmas morning, which was normal, but I knew this time was worse because I had made it worse. Although I was loathe to admit it, it was my own fault. I needed to do something Christmassy, to try to undo some of the damage I had caused by acting like a Scrooge. A Grinchy Scrooge.

It is almost impossible to reflect on Christmas without turning to childhood memories. As I was lying there, a distinct memory popped into my head. Remarkably, it was actually a good Christmas memory.

One Christmas morning when I was still pretty young, a couple of years older than the girls are now, my siblings and I had unwrapped presents, looked in our stockings, and seen the haul that Santa had brought us. Suddenly my dad held up his hand and shushed us all and said, "Listen!"

We all listened, but nobody heard anything. I

remember Mom looking concerned and asking Dad what he'd heard. He just smiled and said, "I think I heard something on the roof! I'm not sure. It sounded kind of like bells, maybe. Jingle bells?"

My younger brother and sister and I jumped up and ran for the door, yelling, "It's Santa!" Mom, looking confused, looked at Dad and shrugged. I saw him wink at her and grin.

I don't remember what we were expecting to see in the bright Arizona daylight, but there was no sleigh, no reindeer, and definitely no Santa.

We all stood on the lawn, disappointed. I turned to look at Dad, but he pointed back to the roof and asked, "Hey, Sammy, what's that?" We all looked, but couldn't see what he wanted us to see. A minute later, Dad took off and then came back from the side of the house with a ladder. He propped it up against the house and said, "Hey, Tiger, are you old enough to climb on the roof?"

I was almost seven at the time, so I wanted my dad to think I was brave. "Sure!" I replied, hiding my nervousness.

Dad held the ladder as I started to climb. I was barefoot, but a single-story house in the Arizona desert rarely encountered hazardous winter conditions. When I got to the top and climbed onto the roof, Dad shouted to me, "Hey, Sammy! What's that over by the chimney?"

I carefully walked across the slope of the roof to the chimney and found an old brown sack made of cloth. My suburban upbringing hadn't given me much exposure to terms like "gunnysack" or "burlap bag." To me it was just an old brown sack.

"Throw it down here, then climb on down. Carefully!" Dad called up. I dropped the bag down to my dad, who caught it. It took me a minute to get my feet right, but then I scampered down the ladder and joined the other kids. Dad patted my back and said, "Good job, Tiger." I loved it when he called me Tiger.

Mom stood chuckling as Dad held up the sack and goaded us, "I wonder where this came from?"

"Santa!"

"Maybe Santa forgot it!"

"Maybe it's more presents!"

"Maybe you should open it!" Mom suggested.

We pulled open the bag and found some scraps of wrapping paper, a few bows, and a string of green, tree-shaped suckers. Nothing much, but we were thrilled. Santa had actually left one of his sacks on OUR roof, and we'd found it! We held tangible proof that Santa had come to our house. All of those faithless schoolyard rumors could now be put to rest.

I do have a faint memory of Mom standing next to Dad and giving him a side hug. He kissed the side of her head and smiled. It was a good memory. But no good Christmas memories seemed to be able to compete with the memory that inevitably would overpower them all, the granddaddy of them all: The very next Christmas, everyone woke up early—except my dad.

2:28 a.m.

As I was busily not sleeping, an idea hit me: just because I didn't care for Christmas didn't mean that I couldn't try and create some Christmas morning magic for my girls. Even if it didn't work, it might earn me some goodwill and forgiveness in the morning

I silently climbed back out of bed and slipped on my sweatpants and t-shirt in the dark. I have a knack for finding my way in the dark, but it drives Amie crazy. Maybe it's because as a kid I believed that eating carrots could help you see in the dark, so I ate a lot of carrots.

Now all I needed was some slippers. I had no idea where mine were. Slippers and I don't get along: I have sweaty feet and, well, you know. Amie has some fuzzy leopard-print slippers that she conveniently leaves just inside the bathroom door. She hates cold tile in the morning. I slipped them on, and I must admit that they were snuggly, but too small. They would do in a pinch. I figured I would only need them for about ten minutes, and she would never even know they were gone.

I went down to the unfinished basement and flailed around for the chain that turns on the only light bulb. What I regard as a basement, most people around here would call a cellar. When I squint, I see the makings of a perfect Man Cave. Eventually.

I looked up and down the wall of wooden shelves, pleased that my memory was right. There on one of the shelves was an old gunnysack left by the previous owners, and probably the five owners previous to them. I pulled it off the shelf and watched as the dust rained down in the light.

There were still some wrapping supplies on the kitchen table, so I grabbed a couple rolls of paper and a few bows and stuffed them in the sack. Now I needed to find a treat. Honestly, I hadn't been paying attention when Amie filled the stockings, so I didn't know what treats Santa brought. Luckily, I did know that Amie had a stash of chocolates hidden in the pantry for what she called "chocolate emergencies." I found an unopened bag of Hershey's Kisses, dropped them into the gunnysack, and outside I went.

2:55 a.m.

This would probably be a good time to stop and tell you about our new-old house, or what happens next might not make much sense. A year earlier, my work had asked me to relocate to Boston. My mom had recently passed, and my brother and sister lived in California, so there was really nothing holding us in Arizona anymore. Amie's parents lived in Colorado, but they were retired and well-off enough that they could hop on a plane and visit whenever they felt like grandparenting.

We packed up and headed to the New England, looking at it as an adventure. After living in an apartment with two little kids in Boston for almost a year, the adventure part was long gone, and we knew it was time to spring for a house. Prices forced us toward the suburbs, and we ended up finding something in Concord. You have probably heard of Concord, as in Lexington-Concord, where the Revolutionary War began in earnest.

Our neighborhood is quiet, with lots of winding roads through a nice, wooded area. The houses aren't too close together, and we both feel that the girls will be able to ride their bikes and play in peace and safety.

The house is easy to describe—give a little kid a crayon and a piece of paper and tell him to draw a house, and it will probably be a fair representation. Two stories, pitched roof, doors in the middle of the ground floor in front and back, and windows around all sides on both floors. It sports brick-red clapboard siding, white shutters, and a rustic wooden door that Amie slapped a wreath on the minute we finished Thanksgiving dinner. (Which, I must admit, looks good.) There is a brick chimney in the middle of the roof that could use some work. There is an attic, filled mostly with dust, whose future is way down on the to-do list.

About fifteen feet from the house, we have a small outbuilding, which, if the door could open, would serve as a nice two-car garage. Until then, we park in front of it on the driveway.

For those of you who are familiar with architecture, I guess it would be called Colonial Revival style. It does look like an old Revolutionary War–era house, but it turns out it was built in the mid-1800s. It all looks fancier than it really is, but it has plenty of room, and lots of opportunity for DIY. This vision comes from watching too many home restoration shows on cable when we were trapped in our tiny apartment with two little ones.

Our plan is to fix it up as we can afford it, doing most of the labor ourselves. It is amazing what you can learn how to do from YouTube. It is fun, and frustrating. Some Saturdays, fixing up the house is the last thing I want to do, but it needs to be done, so I bite my tongue and grab my hammer. I know that eventually it will be very cool and increase the home's value tremendously. For now, it is our new-old house, and we love it, even though it can be drafty. Remember George Bailey's house in *It's a Wonderful Life*? Yeah, that's our situation.

Enough about the house—back to the story.

I went out the back door to get the ladder that I'd left on the deck when I'd torn out the decaying patio cover the previous weekend. I figured that the best place on the roof to toss the Santa bag would be in front, up by the chimney, where it would be visible from the front walkway. I hauled the ladder around the house, careful not to bang it against the wall or gate. It was so quiet out that every sound seemed amplified.

When I'd grabbed Amie's leopard-print slippers, I didn't think that I would be trudging through about two inches of new snow that had fallen that evening. Oops.

I set the ladder on the driveway and leaned it up against the house, but before I could extend it, it began to slip. There was a thin sheet of ice from the rain that had fallen and frozen before it was covered by the new snow. I would need to rethink this.

Instead, I moved toward the center of the house and wedged the legs of the ladder firmly against a brick planter box. It felt much firmer and safer than on the slick driveway. It was a big ladder. Twenty-six feet, to be exact. I knew this because the twenty-foot ladder I'd bought was a few feet short and I'd had to return it, which was a whole 'nother story. This new one, fully extended, was tall enough to prop up against the rain gutter at the top of the roof, with a foot to spare. I ran back around to the deck to grab the gunnysack, feeling the snow fill the slippers. Maybe I could throw them in the dryer?

It was pretty outside, with no moon. The stars were shining, but the clearing clouds had allowed whatever warmth there was to escape. When I started climbing the ladder, that little voice in my head told me it probably wasn't a very good idea. Luckily, I am expert at ignoring that voice. I did think for a second that I should probably go back in and grab a headlamp or a flashlight, some shoes, some gloves, and maybe a coat. This t-shirt wasn't doing such a good job in freezing temperatures.

Sure, I could have gone back inside, but anyone who knows me knows that I'm not wired that way. I figured I could get up the ladder, drop the bag, and be back down quicker than I could get proper gear from inside.

The aluminum ladder rungs were cold on my hands, and the stupid fuzzy slippers were . . . slippery. I took my time and was careful. To be perfectly honest, the older I get, the more I find myself to be afraid of heights. It dawned on me that I was going to have to do this twice, once to place the sack, once to retrieve it. Maybe it wasn't such a great idea. It had never occurred to me before, but Dad probably just tossed the bag on our roof when I was a kid, no ladder needed.

Ah, the beauty of a single-story home.

I climbed high enough that I could see over the edge of the snow-covered roof. The rain gutter was dark and probably filled with leaves frozen in ice. A few shimmering icicles hung from the gutter. When the Christmas lights were on it was a perfect "Christmas look." I probably would have loved this stuff as a kid, a lot more than the neighbor's decorated cactus covered with fake icicles.

All that was left for me to do was to toss the gunnysack up on the roof and climb back down, put everything away, dry the slippers, and go to bed—but, of course, it couldn't possibly be that easy.

I held the sack with my right hand as I clutched the ladder with my left. After a couple practice swings, I swung the bag up and around onto the roof. Almost. The old fabric caught the top corner of the ladder and flew open. The wrapping paper, bows, and candy flew all over the roof, sinking into the new snow, where some of it couldn't be seen at all.

"Dang it!" I said to nobody. Unacceptable. I untangled the gunnysack, tossed it ahead of me, and climbed the last few rungs to where I could crawl onto the roof. Using the gunnysack to keep my hands out of the snow, I successfully crawled onto the roof on all fours, like a dog.

I slowly stood up and got my balance. I should have stayed on my hands and knees. As I took my first step up the steep pitch to retrieve the scattered stuff, I discovered that there was a layer of ice hidden under the snow on the roof, just like on the driveway.

Some people claim that time slows down when they experience an accident or some other type of mishap. Not me. When mine happened, it happened so fast that I had to just lie there and make sense of what was going on.

The whole thing took about three seconds. As I took the first two steps, my back foot slipped on the ice and slid off the roof into the rain gutter. My front foot quickly joined my other foot in the rain gutter, but not before hitting the ladder. My face slammed into the roof, and I felt my nose crunch again, but that was soon to be the least of my worries: About five seconds later, I heard the sound that a twenty-six-foot aluminum extension ladder makes as it slams into a minivan and bounces onto a concrete driveway. The words "arose such a clatter" came immediately to mind.

Oh, man. This was bad.

I realized that I was still slowly slipping, so I gently pushed against the rain gutter with both feet, hoping to find a more secure spot higher up on the roof. Turns out that I wasn't gentle enough: As I pushed, I felt the gutter start to give way, and my body began to slide, feet first, face-down, over the edge. At that moment, I did get a sense of the slow-motion effect, and that only reinforced my belief that this was all she wrote. This was how it would end for me: I would be found in the morning, Christmas morning, and Christmas would be ruined for all of us, forever. Especially me. The irony.

Thankfully the gutter only pulled a foot away from

the roof before it stopped. I knew I couldn't trust it to withstand more pressure, so I shifted as much weight as I could to my torso. I pushed and tried to wiggle back up, but something was holding me back—my foot had entangled with the strand of Christmas lights. I reached down and unwrapped it, which took an agonizingly long time. I then inched my way to safety—the safety of an ice-and-snow-covered, forty-five-degree pitched roof. In the middle of the night. In below-freezing temperatures. Merry Christmas.

It was then I realized two things: My nose was bleeding again—I could taste it—and I only had one slipper on. I made a snowball and held it up to my nose to help staunch the bleeding, but my hand got too cold, so I just pinched my nose while I made my plan.

First, I needed to crawl around and put the stuff back in the gunnysack and lean it against the chimney so it would be visible. I would not be denied. Sure, my circumstances were terrible, but I wasn't going to go through this and NOT pull off some Christmas magic.

I put another snowball up to my nose and took it away. I couldn't see any dark spots, so I figured it had stopped bleeding, but man, did it hurt. I had managed to escape my childhood without ever breaking my nose, and here I was, almost twice on one Christmas Eve.

It took a ridiculous amount of time to collect the wrappings and candy and put the gunnysack in place. First I had to find them in the snow, then dig them out, shake off the snow and return them to the bag. The entire time I knew that it wouldn't take much to start me doing a Bruce Willis *Die Hard* slide off the edge of the building.

With the stuff returned to the gunnysack, I inched my way toward the middle of the roof and propped the sack up against the chimney. I army-man-crawled around the side of the chimney, where I was able to actually sit up and lean my back against the old bricks. I noticed a hint of warmth radiating through the bricks, and it occured to me that this was leftover heat from the fire downstairs. For the first time since that first slip, I felt somewhat safe, and the adrenaline began to subside. As the shock and stress diminished, I became acutely aware of how crazy cold I was. My hands were almost numb, and my slipperless foot was feeling the pins and needles of being wet and cold. Really cold.

I switched the slipper over to my cold foot, then turned and pressed my bare foot up against the chimney to try and warm it up. Somewhat proud of my resourcefulness, I lay back and started thinking.

3:30 a.m., or thereabouts

What options did I have?

My first thought was to call 9-1-1 and ask for help. Simple enough, except for the tiny fact that I had left my phone on the mantel in the family room.

I could scream for help, but I already knew that Amie was out cold with her earplugs blocking out whatever noise I might make, and besides, she was on the other end of the house on the ground floor. The girls were on the second floor, directly above our bedroom, but I seriously doubted they would hear, let alone process what was going on, and again, wrong end of the house.

What about the neighbors? What neighbors? We were the last house on the street. The nearest house was probably three hundred yards away and belonged to the Simms. Normally they might be able to hear me yell, but considering they were spending Christmas on a Caribbean cruise, I knew well enough to save my lungs and voice.

I could climb down. Except just the previous weekend I'd torn down the old wooden awning covering the deck. There were no dormers, ledges, or window sills that I might be able to reach, and even if I could, who knew if they would be covered with snow and ice, or if they would bear my weight? We lived in a box. A big rectangular box. Even Spiderman would have been hard-pressed to find a way to climb down. I take that back. Spidey would simply climb down the rain gutter downspout like it was no big deal. I'm not Spiderman.

I could try and jump across to the garage. I turned and looked to see if it was realistic. The jump would be about fifteen feet over, but also ten feet down. I could jump across and down, land on the sloped roof of the garage, slide off, and drop the remaining ten feet to the ground. It thought it might be doable, until I remembered that there was no way to get a running start. I stared at the divide and accepted what a laughably bad idea it would be for anyone that isn't named Tom Cruise.

Or, I could wait until morning, and eventually someone should come looking for me. That was the first thought that really made me feel queasy inside. Up until then, I hadn't really felt nervous, but I could feel the anxiety building. I figured it was probably getting close to four a.m., so it would still be several hours before anyone noticed I was gone. Even a thin-blooded desert-dweller like me knows that hypothermia would set in well before the sun came up. A t-shirt, one fuzzy slipper, and sweatpants are no match for freezing temperatures. Even if I survived, I figured I would probably lose some toes or fingers to frostbite.

I decided I needed to be patient and process the

bizarreness of the situation before I attempted anything stupid.

Waiting was the worst. I had absolutely no concept of how quickly time was passing. What felt like hours was probably just minutes. I was left alone with my thoughts, which quickly returned to my dad's last Christmas.

When I say that he didn't wake up early on Christmas morning that year, I mean that he didn't wake up. At all.

Our family tradition required that on Christmas morning, we kids would wait in our rooms until my parents were up. Dad would go downstairs, start a fire in the fireplace, turn on the tree and put on some music while Mom got ready to face the morning. Then Dad would make a loud show of coming down the hall to get us.

"Looks like someone's been here!

"I don't see any lumps of coal! You guys must have been awfully nice this year."

Meanwhile, we were losing our minds with anticipation.

Finally, Dad would open our doors. The three of us would line up and march into the family room as Mom videotaped our reactions to what Santa had left.

One morning—that morning—while we waited in our rooms, we heard doors open and close, voices of strangers, and what sounded like crying. After what seemed like forever, Mom came in. Her face was flushed and wet with tears and she was shaking. She gathered us around her and through sobs explained to us that Daddy had had a heart attack in his sleep and had died during the night, and that he was gone to be with Jesus and Heavenly Father.

I refused to believe her. I pulled away and ran out of my room down the hall. I ran into a police officer standing in front of my parents' room. I tried to run around him, but he gently picked me up and carried me back to my mom.

I don't remember much about the rest of that Christmas Day. It remains a blur. I'm not even sure if we opened presents or not. I know that I don't remember what Santa brought me that year. From that point on, I never cared about anything Christmas. Since then, Christmas has never been a magical time for me, but more of a necessary evil, full of grief and anger that I can't wait to get past. My anger was never directed at my dad, because I know he got cheated like we did. Instead, I wasn't too happy with God, or Jesus for that matter. Better said, I was angry at both of them, which brought all sorts of other, less charitable emotions to the forefront of any Christmas celebration.

I try not to bring it up, but it hovers over me during the holidays like Eeyore's dark cloud. Christmas, for me, has become something I endure rather than celebrate. I used to try harder to put on a show and act like everything was great, but I had gotten lazy as of late. I knew that my "I hate Christmas" vibe was bleeding over into other areas of my life, even my relationship with Amie.

This was going to be a long, sleepless night—but not for the reason I thought. I didn't want to spend another minute, alone with my thoughts, on this roof. I needed to figure out how to get down.

The simplest idea was to just throw caution to the wind and jump. To make it less dangerous, I figured I could slide down the roof headfirst, grab onto the rain gutter, and then slide off, hoping the gutter would slow the fall. Or I could try to land on the car, but I've seen too many movies to want to fall onto a parked car. It always seems to happen to the villains. Even worse than that fate would be surviving and having to explain to my wife and the insurance company that the car was damaged because I jumped off the roof.

I psyched myself into believing that jumping was the way to go. Besides, it was only twenty feet. Well, more like twenty-three feet, because the first floor was a couple feet above ground because of the basement. I was still a young man, and could jump twenty-three feet and land without killing myself. Right? Maybe?

Sure, there was always the off chance that I could sprain an ankle. Or break an ankle. Or a leg. Or my back. Or my skull. Or worse.

I crawled from my secure spot near the chimney to the edge of the roof and looked down. I could see the white snow below, but I couldn't make out what it covered, except where it was obviously concrete. If I jumped in the right place, I could land on a bush to break my fall. Of course, I could just as easily land on a sprinkler pipe sticking up in that bush and impale myself. That image would make for a lovely Christmas memory for my young family.

Maybe I could swing down enough to kick in one of the windows and climb inside? Or maybe grab one of the window shutters and work my way down, you know, like in the movies? It was becoming more and more apparent that I watch too many movies.

I closed my eyes and took a mental stroll around the house. The back yard was worse than the front because of all the deck work. The side yards had fences and gates and a longer drop from the roof. Besides, if I landed badly, it was a long way to drag myself to the front door—which was most likely locked.

I made up my mind. The best choice was to go for the front yard, by hanging onto the rain gutter as long as it would support me, then timing my release to land on the lawn.

"You can do this!" I said, just to hear the words.

4:20 a.m.–ish

My heart was racing and my adrenaline surged to where I wasn't paying attention to the cold. I was too busy psyching myself up for the jump. My head was hanging off the roof, looking down. I reached out and gripped the rain gutter with both hands as tightly as my cold fingers would allow and began to turn my body to let my legs to go first. It was slippery and scary.

I was in position, with my body lying along the edge of the roof. All I needed to do was swing my legs off the edge and . . .

"Stop!"

The voice was loud enough that it startled me. I stuck my head back over the edge and looked down. There was no one there. Let's try this again. I pulled my head back and got ready to go.

"Stop!" The voice came again. "Don't do this."

Now, as I mentioned, I have a voice in my head that occasionally tells me what to do. Even earlier that night it had pestered me into waking up Amie to apologize, and to scrap the ladder idea. Come to think of it, I would have been better off listening to the voice both times.

But this voice was different. It was powerful. Adamant. And I knew it wasn't mine.

"Who are you?"

Silence.

"Who are you, and why are you talking to me?"

Nothing.

I let go of the gutter and rolled onto my back.

"Was that you, God?"

Still nothing, which was usually how it went when I tried talking to God.

I stared up at the night sky and wondered if there really had been a voice, or if I was hearing things that weren't really there. I knew from watching Nat Geo that one of the signs of hypothermia can be hallucinations. That was probably it. Besides, God had not made it a practice of chatting with me. Ever.

But this voice was different. It was somehow familiar, yet it was impossible to tell where it came from, unless, of course, it merely came from my imagination.

I crawled back up to my safe place by the chimney to try and make sense of it. I thought through my limited options again and decided that jumping was still the most logical way down. Besides, when I was a young man I wouldn't have hesitated. I'd jumped off fifty-foot cliffs at the lake, and had jumped off the roof of our house into our pool countless times. Granted, I was landing in water, not the frozen stuff below. Frankly, if there had been a decent snowdrift, I would have given it a go much sooner.

The cold was messing with me, and I knew I needed to act. I rubbed my hands together to create some friction, then stuck them under my armpits. I needed to warm them up if I was going to trust them to grab the rain gutter and hold on.

Feeling as ready as I was ever going to feel, I left the security of the chimney and started crawling, army-man-style, toward the edge. I had only moved a few feet when the voice came at me again. The same voice. The same calm intensity. The same familiarity.

"Don't do this." It went on to confirm my doubts: "You can't see where you'll land, or what is under the snow."

I stopped and rolled on my back again. I wasn't happy with the intrusion. "Hey! Whoever you are, if you don't want me to jump, you better give me something better to try."

No response.

But I took it seriously, and crawled back to the chimney. Every time I crawled, I got more snow in my clothes. Some of it melted, some of it froze. I knew hypothermia was not far off.

After another almost-out-of-control slide, I managed to return to my position at the chimney and put my bare foot back up against the bricks. This time I sat and waited. Time was lost to me. There was no moon to see by, and the only expectation I had was that eventually the sky would begin to brighten in the east. Unfortunately, I didn't know if that would be soon or hours from now.

I began to feel very tired. Even though I knew that falling asleep was a terrible, dangerous thing to do, I couldn't keep my head up. I found myself doing that head bob thing we do when trying to stay awake in church.

A voice started pushing its way through my sleep. At first it was quiet, then got louder.

"Wake up. Wake up!" the voice said. "You can't sleep—you won't wake up if you do."

That startled me for a moment, but I soon found myself nodding off yet again.

"Tiger, wake up!"

My eyes flew open. I had never been so awake in my life.

"Dad?"

I rubbed my eyes and stammered, "Is . . . is that you?"

"Yes it is, Sammy. You must stay awake."

"How? What? Why?" My mouth couldn't express the myriad questions racing through my head. "Am I hearing things? Is this a hallucination?"

"I don't expect that you are seeing things, but what you are hearing is not a hallucination. It is real. It's me."

"How is this possible . . . you are . . ."

"Dead? About that. You know all the things you learned in church, about how we are all eternal beings, and how there is a God?"

"I remember."

"It's true. It's all true. He is real. We are eternal. I died, but I am still alive in a different place."

My head was spinning as I tried to process what I

was hearing, how I was hearing it and who was saying it. I didn't know how to react, so I reacted in the most honest way I could—I put my head in my hands and burst into tears. Big ugly sobs wracked my body. I don't know where they came from—I guess I had been holding them back for most of my life. I mean, how do you get your head around something like this?

It took me a couple of minutes to gain control. "Have you been watching me all these years?"

"No. It doesn't really work like that, but tonight is different. I guess you could call it a special circumstance, an inflection point."

"Don't say that. It sounds like I am going to die and you are here to get me."

The voice answered in a familiar, quiet way that tore at my heart. "No, I'm here to make sure that doesn't happen."

"What? Like you are my guardian angel?"

"Not so much a guardian angel, but someone who has a personal interest in seeing you get out of this mess alive."

"Can I call you Clarence?" I can be such a dork.

My other-worldly, disembodied father's voice laughed out loud. "Hah! I'm not a guardian angel, and I don't need to get my wings. You are seriously making movie jokes at a time like this?"

"A time like this? How bad is it?"

"It could be pretty bad, but let's see what we can do to avoid it."

"Can I just jump already? You keep stopping me."

"Not yet. There are things that need to be taken care of first."

The cryptic remark sailed over my head, as I wasn't thinking too clearly. Given the ridiculousness of my situation, and the heavenly involvement, you can understand my confusion.

"What do I need to take care of?"

"Let's talk."

"Okay, but wait, I have a question. Can you watch me anytime, like when I'm in the bathroom? Because that is really creepy if you can."

"No. It doesn't work that way." I could remember the familiar notes of my dad's exasperation. "I need you to focus, Son."

"Okay . . ."

"First, I've missed you. So has your mom."

"What?" I almost jumped to my feet. "You're with Mom?"

"Of course! I waited for her for a long time."

"Eighteen years. How is she?"

"Eighteen? That does sound like a lot, but time is a funny thing here; it passes much more quickly. She is terrific. So good to have her back." Dad stopped for a second. "Sorry, we are getting off track here. I can't stay long, so we need to get on task."

Man, that sounded like my dad. He was a hard worker and had taught me to work at an early age. I guess it shouldn't have surprised me that he was still task-driven in the afterlife.

"So, I'm hoping that there's more to heaven than

floating around on clouds, playing the harp."

"You have no idea, but hopefully you'll have to wait to learn more about that. You ready?"

I rubbed my hands together some more and stuck them under my armpits. My foot was going numb. "Yeah, let's get to it—whatever 'it' is. I'm almost frozen."

"Okay. First, tell me about Amie."

"Amie? What about her?"

"Remember, I never knew her. Tell me about her."

"Well, she has brown eyes . . ."

"Hang on!" he interrupted. "I don't care what she looks like. Tell me *about* her."

I thought for a moment before proceeding. "Amie is amazing. She's a great mom. She takes care of our girls so well she makes it look easy. It's like there isn't anything she can't do. Some days I'll come home from work and she'll have ripped out a bookshelf and be building something in its place."

My dad interrupted, "I can tell you this—your mom thought Amie was great and really loves her."

"Yeah, so do I. She's just a really good person, and she's very kind to everyone. Her goodness comes from inside, like she's just naturally that way. I have to think about it. She just does it."

"Keep going."

"Um, she is funny—she can't tell a lie to save her life. I suppose that is a good thing. Even if she tries to lie to me, I can spot it a mile away. Somebody once told her that she has no guile, which is accurate."

"That is very high praise. How do you feel about her?"

"Well, I love her. She is the single best thing that has ever happened to me. I can't imagine my life without her. Scratch that—I don't want to imagine my life without her. Without her, none of it would make any sense for me. And she puts up with a tremendous amount of crap from me."

"Has she ever heard you say that?"

His question caught me off guard. "Of course . . . maybe . . . I don't know." The memory of how I'd left her, crying and alone on Christmas Eve, flooded back into my mind and convicted me.

"Probably not. I'm not as romantic as I used to be."

"Do you think it's romance she's looking for?"

"I doubt it. She would probably appreciate it if I were less grumpy and helped her more around the house. The girls are a handful, and I'll admit, sometimes I just ignore the chaos until she takes care of it."

"Hmmm," was all he said, so I continued.

"She really loves Christmas, and I know it makes her sad that I despise it."

"Despise what?"

"Christmas. I'm not a fan."

"Yeah, we're gonna have to come back to that. Tell me about the girls."

"Gracie is three, and she's a cutie. Looks a lot like Amie, but with curlier hair. She is at a really fun stage. She loves animals and coloring." I could feel my mood and countenance brightening as I talked about her.

"And Sarah?"

I paused for a minute, struck that he obviously knew their names. He must have noticed my odd reaction because he quickly added, "Your mom told me about them, and how adorable they are. Go on."

"Yeah, Mom had a soft spot for Sarah. She is five, very strong-willed..."

"Like her father?"

"Yeah," I chuckled. "Or maybe it skipped a generation and she's like her grandfather. But she's really sweet. Seems to have Amie's knack for making people around her happy. She's a lot like Mom that way, and I think Mom loved her extra for it. She's an interesting mix of a very gentle soul and a determined kid. She never gives us any problems."

I instinctively rubbed my nose, remembering that not long ago I'd left her in tears after we'd bonked heads. "Yeah, I could have handled that better."

"Handled what better?"

"Nothing." I pressed on. "The girls are great, Amie is great, I am a blessed man."

"What do you think they would say about you if I asked them?" he asked.

Ouch. Not sure I wanted to go there, but I was starting to think that my dad had a fairly good idea already. "I think they know that I will take care of them and that I work hard, but they would probably rather I work less, even if it means providing less. They're too young to understand that stuff. They think I'm fun, but honestly, they are probably a little afraid of me."

"That's a big concession. Why would your daughters be afraid of their dad?"

"I don't know. Hey, I'm really freezing. We about done?" I was deflecting.

My dad didn't respond.

"Look, I can be a lot of fun, but I can also be kind of cranky, especially at this time of year. I think it makes them nervous because I'm unpredictable and they don't know what version of Dad they're gonna get. I don't ever get violent or loud, but I can get pretty intense. Amie calls it my 'Hell Look.'"

"Well that sounds lovely. Go on."

"They know I love them, and I know they love me. I should probably spend more time with them, just playing and stuff. I have to work a lot."

"Do you need to work a lot?"

I'd fudged the truth just a tiny bit and Dad had nailed me on it.

"Honestly? I don't have to work as much as I do. Sometimes I stay longer than I need to, or find other things to do so I can come home later, after the girls are in bed. After working all day, the last thing I want to do is dishes and bath time."

As I said those words out loud, I sounded like a complete jerk. Worst husband ever. I was embarrassed—no, ashamed—to be telling my dad these things. What kind of crappy father and husband would do that sort of thing?

I guess my father was thinking the same thing. "If

I could do it all over again—"

"You what? You wouldn't have a heart attack? Right."

"No. I had no control over that. What I was going to say, before you interrupted me, is that if I could do it over again, I would have spent every possible moment with you kids and your mom. I had no idea it would be cut so short."

Revisting my dad's death with my dad right there set me off again. The ugly tears were back. If this was a hallucination, then it was way too personal. I wasn't ready to handle this kind of thing, but Dad seemed to be.

"Grab those girls tight and don't let go. You have no idea how much time you have left. You have so much yet to do."

I grasped at the flicker of hope. "So you are saying that this isn't it? That I'm going to survive this?"

The voice was silent.

"Dad? Are you still there?"

"Yes."

"You messed up, didn't you? You weren't supposed to tell me that this was not the end. I was supposed to think I might die tonight! Uh oh, hope you don't get in trouble. Looks like you lost your leverage, Clarence."

"Are you always this cynical?" Dad responded.

I thought for a moment. "No, I'm not very cynical, except when it comes to religious stuff."

"How so?"

"Losing your dad—your best friend—at eight

years old can cause you to look at a kind and loving God with different eyes. I'm still what you would call religious: we take the girls to church, we pray together, teach the girls scripture stories, say grace, etc. I'm not faithless."

"But . . . ?"

"But sometimes I feel like I'm just going through the motions. Especially when I get to the point where I pray—I feel like my prayers can't make it past the ceiling."

"Does talking with me change your perspective?"

"I guess it does, but it doesn't change how I feel." He didn't respond, leaving me to continue. "Look, Dad. I struggled for a lot of years after you died. It was hard, and it was unfair. I was mad at God for a long time."

"And now?"

"Now?" I had to think about that one. "I guess I am still angry—if not bitter. I will say that having the girls, and Amie, has helped soften me a little."

"I imagine God would be okay with that."

"With what?"

"With you being angry at Him. He would probably rather have you angry than atheistic. I mean, your dad was taken away far too early. So, let's count that as a partial victory. And for the record, God loves you anyway."

Leave it to my dad to find a way to make my anger toward God a positive thing. "I never thought of it that way. I guess I haven't really slipped as far as I thought."

We were both quiet for a moment, and my mind went back to how cold I was, and how I could no longer feel my unslippered toes. I think Dad sensed that. "Hey, we need to wind this up, but I do have one last question."

I had no pride or vanity left. "Shoot."

"Why do you hate Christmas?"

"Wait. Ask that again." I jammed my fingers into my ears.

"Why do you hate Christmas?" he repeated. "And why are you doing that?"

"I can still hear you with my fingers in my ears. That means that you are inside my head. Are you a hallucination?"

"I told you before, this is not a hallucination. And the reason you can hear me without your ears is that this conversation is happening inside of you."

"In my head?"

"In your head, in your heart, in your soul," he said. "But I can't read your mind."

"So this is a spirit-to-spirit thing?"

"Yes, exactly, but I can see you, and I can see that you are deflecting again. Why do you hate Christmas?"

"Hate is a strong word," I said. "I just don't get it. People start stressing out about it before Halloween is even over, and then skip right past Thanksgiving. It has just gotten out of hand."

"Then you are saying that you don't like Christmas because other people do?"

"No! You don't get it. It's all about money and

gifts and decorations and stuff. It's so commercialized that it doesn't really mean anything anymore."

"Do you get it?"

I interrupted. I was on a roll. "To make it even worse, it's totally secularized now. You can't even talk about Jesus anymore, and it's supposed to be about His birth. Instead it's all Santa and snowmen and stuff. I don't think the kids are even allowed to sing songs that have any religious overtones in school anymore. It's all 'Season's Greetings' and 'Happy Holidays' because the secular world is afraid to say 'Merry Christmas.'"

I realized that I was waving my hands around and talking too loudly. If someone had seen me from the street, they would have thought I had lost my mind. This gave me pause to consider that perhaps I had lost my mind. It was too weird, so I stopped venting.

My father must have thought it was weird, too, as he left me with my thoughts. I calmed down, stuck my freezing hands back under my arms, and waited. A couple minutes later, he was back.

"Are you finished?" he responded with that calm, authoritative voice that I remembered from my childhood. I figured once a father . . .

"Yes."

"It sounds like you think the world has it wrong."

"Yes."

"Perhaps the world does have it wrong. Instead of talking about the world, let's talk about you."

"What about me?"

"For starters, why are you up here on the roof in

the middle of the night, freezing to death?"

"Because the roof was slippery, and I accidentally knocked the ladder down, and then you stopped me from jumping. Twice."

"That is all true, but not what I'm asking. I want you to tell me why you came up here in the first place."

He had me. I could sense his trap a mile away, but it made no sense to be anything but honest. "I came up here to try and share a little bit of Christmas magic with my girls—like you did for us—and I screwed it up."

"Let me see if I have this right. Your hate for Christmas, and disdain for Santa and gifts and all that 'stuff' runs so deep that you climbed up here in the middle of the night to help reinforce the magic of Christmas and Santa for your girls? That makes no sense."

"Yeah, I know. What can I say?"

"That maybe you are not so committed to your Christmas hate as you might profess?"

"Maybe. Oh, alright. I still want the girls to love Christmas. I want them to enjoy the magic and the fun like I did when I was a kid. Well, until . . . "

"So, then, why the rant?" He had a knack for nailing me with the perfect question.

Usually I am pretty quick with a response—usually more spontaneous than well-thought-out. In this instance, I truly did not have an answer. I could see the paradox, but I couldn't explain it.

"I dunno, habit?" I said. "I'm open for suggestions."

"That's for you to figure out. I have confidence in you, Sammy. You'll work through it."

"You're leaving," I said, more as a statement than a question.

"Yes. Morning is coming, and I'll leave you to it."

"To what? Death before sunrise?"

"No. You'll be alright."

"But how? How will I be alright? I'm still stuck up here, but now I'm freezing and my mind is racing."

"You'll be alright," he repeated. "I am so glad I could spend some time with you, despite the circumstances."

He was leaving me. Again. I could feel the hot streak of a tear contrast against my cold cheek. "I could sure use a hug right about now. Do you really have to go?"

"I do. This was a very rare and unique experience. We get to peek in once in a while to see how things are going down here, but not often, and usually just for major events. Interacting is a distinct rarity reserved for crisis."

"Crisis? Am I in a crisis?"

"I would think so. But not the kind you are thinking of. It's not about the roof. It's about this being an inflection point in your life, and what happens after."

"That's fair, but how am I going to get down?"

"You have everything you need to find your answers. I've gotta go. I love you, Tiger."

"I love you, too. Thanks, Dad, for everything. Not just for now, but for everything. And please tell Mom I love her and I miss her."

"Will do." And he was gone.

I could feel his presence leave me. I don't know that I have ever felt as alone in my entire life as I did at that moment. My hands and feet were freezing, and my mind was jumbled, and honestly, I was scared. Not just about my predicament, but about everything: my life, my faith, my wife, my kids . . . my soul.

5:00 a.m. - Maybe?

My dad's visit had just confirmed all of the religious teachings that I had learned when I was a child. The same beliefs that had become much less of a priority in my life the older I got. Now, suddenly, I knew for a certainty that there was an afterlife. That my parents were still alive—sure, in another place or dimension or whatever, but they still existed. How does one process that?

As my mind whirled, I remembered something my dad had said that had gotten lost in the goodbyes: "You have everything you need to find your answers."

But I didn't have *anything*—or so I thought. Then I remembered. I stuck my cold hand in the pocket of my sweats and fished out two things: the carved baby Jesus and the angel from the Nativity set that I had repossessed from Gracie's room. I leaned back against the chimney and put one piece in each hand and mulled them over as I sat in the darkness.

How could these little pieces of wood answer any of my questions? Baby Jesus? I was never one to think too much about baby Jesus because it seemed to me that the grown-up Jesus is where things got real. Partly to humor my dad, and partly out of desperation, I squeezed that little wooden piece and closed my eyes.

I thought of how on that sacred night over two thousand years ago, God sent his Son down to earth to be born, and how He couldn't have picked a more humble circumstance. Nothing like my kids sleeping warmly in their beds. In my mind I started quoting what I could of the Christmas story from Luke, Chapter 2, in the Bible. I was surprised by how much I remembered: Mary, Joseph, the angel, the shepherds, all of it. If I am being completely honest, the reason I knew the story so well was not because of my disciplined religious studies, but because I'd watched *A Charlie Brown Christmas* a hundred times as a kid when it came out on DVD. I can't even think through the Christmas story without hearing it in Linus's voice.

I thought of Christ as He ministered to people. Casting out devils, healing the sick, teaching, comforting, loving. I could feel my pulse begin to retreat, and a new calm came over me.

I thought about His struggles as He taught, how He courageously confronted those who needed it, and showed tender mercy to those who needed that. I thought of Him cleansing the temple, yet gently teaching the woman at the well. I thought of Him walking on the water, and patiently training His disciples.

I thought of the last week of His life, as He returned to Jerusalem. I thought of His last meeting with His apostles, and how they ate the bread and drank the wine. I thought of them singing together before they left into that crucial night.

I thought of Him kneeling in the Garden of Gethsemane. Kneeling, suffering, pleading with His Father to rescue Him.

I thought of his enemies confronting Him and taking Him prisoner at the same time He was healing one of those very soldiers.

I thought of Him being interrogated, whipped, spat upon. I thought of Him crucified on the cross.

I thought of Him appearing to Mary the next morning. I imagined the joy that she and the others must have felt to know that He was still alive! This meant more to me in that moment that ever before.

By this time I no longer felt cold. My mind was consumed by my thoughts of Jesus. I had spent much of my life learning about Christ. I was fully committed to my faith, but I'd never felt like I knew Him *personally*. My entire life I'd heard people talking about what they called their "relationship" with Jesus. I didn't get it, and not getting it caused me angst. I don't know when I stopped trying to find Him, but I know that when I did, my faith became more about what I had to do, what list I needed to check off, rather than about loving Christ. I walked the walk, and talked the talk, but I always felt a bit like an imposter.

Maybe . . . maybe that was an underlying reason for my disdain for all things Christmas. Could it be that I hated Christmas because, deep inside, I didn't really believe it?

A feeling surged inside me as I had that thought. As cheesy as it sounds, the thought strongly came to me that I needed to pray about it. So I did.

I got on my knees, steadied myself, closed my eyes and pressed my forehead against the brick chimney. I begin to pray out loud, because I knew nobody could hear me. I don't know how long I spent on my knees on the roof. It might have been minutes, it might have been an hour. What I do know is what happened.

It was not a formal prayer. It came from a deeper, more desperate place. I needed to know two things: if God was there, and if He would forgive me. Not for any grave sins I had committed, but for just going through the motions and not fully giving Him my heart.

I pleaded for forgiveness. For not trusting Him. For not loving Him. For being angry with Him. I begged for His mercy. I begged Him for another chance.

Repenting. Yes, I guess I was repenting. As I did, I felt the angst begin to leave and the turmoil fade from my mind and heart. It was slowly, gently replaced with a peace I was not familiar with, and an unexpected warmth coursed through my body, overpowering the freezing air. I felt. . . `loved, and somehow less broken.

As the tears trickled down my face, I next thought of my sweet Amie, and how I had pulled away from her. I was being honest when I told my dad that she was the very best thing that ever happened to me, and what I had given her in return was a sullen attitude and grief. My heart filled with a new, profound love for her. I know it was bolstered with my newfound understanding that our potential to be together forever was not merely a trite teaching or the stuff of romantic songs, but a reality.

I committed then and there to treat her in a way that would cause her to *want* to spend eternity with me, because lately, I think that she would take a pass.

Gracie and Sarah were probably twenty feet away from where I knelt, and I wanted nothing more than to hug them and kiss them. To tell them stories and protect them, to instill in their hearts what I was feeling about our Savior, to love them like He loves us.

I opened my eyes and sat back and took a deep breath.

Wow.

Sorry, but that is the only word I can think of to describe what I experienced. Wow. I wished my dad could check in for an update so I could share it with him, but somehow I felt he already knew.

I realized that I was still clenching my fists. I slowly opened my hands and saw the baby Jesus and the angel, and I put the Jesus figurine back in my pocket.

The angel. What was I supposed to do with this?

I wracked my brain thinking about scripture stories that involved angels. I chuckled when my first thought was the angel's standoff with Balaam's talking donkey—a classic.

I thought about the times that angels visited Jesus's earthly dad to warn him to flee to Egypt, and then to come back home. That suddenly meant more to me than it had before.

I thought about the angels that ministered to Jesus after the Devil tempted Him, and when He suffered in the Garden of Gethsemane.

I thought of the Christmas angel visiting Mary and Joseph, and announcing the big news to the shepherds.

I paused. The angel announcing to the shepherds. Was there something there? I squeezed the wooden angel in my hand and thought. I was close, but didn't have the answer yet. I said a silent prayer, "Please, God, help me figure out how to get off this roof."

The answer came immediately: *Angels make announcements.* They call down, or come down, from heaven and announce things to people who need to hear them. That was it!

I carefully stood up, put the figurine back into my pocket, and looked at the chimney. I knew I had to think this through carefully, because if I got the sequence wrong, I could still die up here.

5:40 a.m. Approximately.

Cupping my hands around my mouth, I leaned over and shouted down the chimney as loud as I could:

"Hey, Com-pooo-ter, turn on the exterior lights."

I looked at the edge of the roof and saw the glow of the multi-colored Christmas lights flicker on!

"Yes!" I shouted to no one, and pumped my fist in the air.

Next, "Hey, Com-pooo-ter, turn on the Christmas tree." I scooted a bit closer to the edge of the roof and was thrilled to see the soft glow of the Christmas tree lights shining onto the snow from the family room window. Back to the chimney.

I cupped my hands again and began to shout, but caught myself. That was close. I thought it through one more time and then shouted into the chimney, "Hey, Com-pooo-ter, speakers at volume ten."

There was no response or any way to tell if the stereo was even on, but I didn't remember turning it off. Here goes nothing . . .

"Hey, Com-pooo-ter, play 'Up on the Housetop' from playlist Christmas." I put my ear over the chimney and could hear a most beautiful sound: Christmas music.

And it was LOUD.

I carefully dragged myself to the edge of the roof and stuck my head over to watch below. Within minutes I saw another light come on, then another. Then the music went quiet.

I shouted at the ground, "Amie! I'm outside!"

Nothing. I shouted again. This time I saw another light go on—the girls' room.

Another shout, still no response. "C'mon!" I thought.

Suddenly the front porch light turned on, and I heard the door open. It was Amie. My Amie. My heart swelled with love for this woman like it never had before. Not because she was going to save me, but because she was going to be mine, forever.

Before I could say anything, she walked out and went straight into the yard, where she bent down and picked up her fuzzy slipper and shook the snow off of it.

"Sorry about that," I said calmly.

Amie looked up at me in disbelief and pulled her bathrobe tightly around her. "What in the world are you doing up there, and why do you have my slippers? Get down! You'll freeze to death."

I let the irony pass and said, "I'm sorry, and I'll explain everything to you, but first, go get the girls."

"Get the girls? Are you serious? It's, like, almost six in the morning."

"They're already up." I said. "I saw their light go on."

At that moment, the front door flew open and both girls ran out on the porch. "Mommy, why are you outside? And why was the music so loud?"

"Hey, girls!" I interrupted before Amie could answer. "I heard something in the night up on the roof, so I came up to investigate."

I'm not sure if the little girls or Amie had a bigger expression of disbelief.

"Run back inside and put your boots on, then come back out." I shouted. The girls raced back inside.

Amie had her hands on her hips, with an incredulous look on her face. "I don't even know where to begin."

"I know, and I'll explain everything. Promise."

"Sam, are you okay? I mean, is something weird going on?"

"Oh, no, no. I'm okay. Cold, but great."

The girls came back wearing boots and nightgowns.

"Hang on a second," I shouted.

I worked my way back up to the chimney and grabbed the gunnysack, then returned to the edge of the roof. "Look what I found!" I said, as I tossed the sack onto the ground in front of them.

The girls were all over it, emptying it out and finding the candy within seconds. Amie looked more baffled than ever. The girls weren't curious at all. Santa had left something on the roof, and Dad had found it. Completely understandable in a three- and five-year-old's world.

"Honey, I need help getting down. Could you maybe stand the ladder back up? I kinda knocked it over."

Amie stared for a second, then jumped into action. She walked to the driveway and picked up the end of the ladder. "You know you dented the minivan, right?"

"I know, and I'm sorry."

"I can't wait to hear you explain this. What should I do?" she asked.

"Make sure the foot of the ladder is wedged in the planter so that it won't slip, then try and lift it up and prop it against the house. Eventually you can extend it up to the roof."

"You're serious?"

"Desperately."

Amie did exactly as I instructed, and within a couple of minutes she had the ladder two-thirds of the way up the wall, but then we ran into a glitch: When the ladder had fallen, the supports that let the ladder extend had broken, leaving it a good ten feet short.

"I don't know what to do! Should I call 9-1-1?" she asked. "Let me get my phone."

"Not yet. Give me a second to think about it."

As I was thinking, that calm, familiar voice came back into my head—or my soul, "Hey Tiger. I'm proud of you. It looks like you will be okay."

"Thanks, Dad, but I still don't know how to get down."

"Jump."

I couldn't help but laugh, "Jump? You've gotta be kidding me!"

"Now you can see where you are landing and Amie is there to help you. More importantly, you are now ready to jump. It wasn't the right time before. You had too much to do."

"My original plan?"

"Yes, that would work just fine."

"Thanks, Dad—and Merry Christmas."

"Merry Christmas to you, Sammy."

I heard Amie's voice shouting, "Who are you talking to?"

"I'll explain later." I shouted back down to Amie, "Everybody go stand by the door, I'm going to jump."

Amie didn't move. "No way. You are not jumping off that roof."

"It will be fine. I promise. You will just have to trust me."

Amie put up her hands to protest, but then lowered them. She was probably still upset at me from last night and figured, "Whatever. Sam's gonna do what Sam's gonna do."

I turned my body sideways, made sure I was clear of the Christmas lights, reached out and grabbed the dangling rain gutter as tightly as I could with my almost-frozen hands, and slid off the roof.

My body weight pulled against the rain gutter, pulling it gradually from the edge of the roof. As it pulled away, it swung me out a few feet over where I knew there was nothing but lawn. Another section of gutter pulled away, dropping me down another five feet, then ten.

My hands gave out and I lost my grip on the rain gutter. I fell, but only for a moment. I landed on my feet, on the lawn. It looked so easy.

Amie and the girls rushed out to me in the snow, Amie was not pleased, but I have never been happier to see anyone in my entire life. She started to say something, but couldn't as I grabbed her in a bear hug and held on tight. The girls each grabbed a leg and help on while chanting, "Santa came! Santa came!"

Amie pulled back and gave me a panicked look. "Sam, how long have you been out here? You're cold as ice, and your hair is frozen."

"A few hours. I'm not sure."

"Should we take you to the hospital, or call an ambulance?"

"Not yet. Just help me inside and maybe grab me a blanket?"

Amie wrapped her arm around my waist and helped me walk. My nearly-frozen feet didn't provide much balance. She glanced down at them, one still covered in leopard and said, "So that's where my other slipper went. You, Mister, have some serious explaining to do."

"I know, I know. And I'll tell you everything as soon as I'm able. Right now, some dry clothes and a hot chocolate sounds great."

My angel wife turned to me with an expression of confusion and fear. "Sam, is everything okay? I don't understand what is happening."

I pulled her close, "Everything is more than okay. Everything is wonderful—or at least it will be. It might take a little time, but I'll get there. I promise. Oh, and Merry Christmas, and I'm so sorry."

She pulled away, rightfully skeptical. "Merry Christmas? Don't mock me."

I pulled her back, tighter than ever, kissed her forehead and whispered in her ear, "Merry Christmas, my love, and I mean it with all my heart and soul."

Looking up into the heavens, I winked, and softly whispered, "Thanks, Dad—and thank you, Jesus."

THE END

ABOUT THE AUTHOR

Bradley McBride has been blogging for more than a decade, currently at www.ThusWeSee.com. Bradley's talent is taking complex, deep doctrine and breaking it down to present it in a way that is understandable, entertaining and makes you want to read more. He specializes in walking the precarious tightrope between humor and spirituality in his writing. He loves to teach, to learn and to laugh.

Up on the Housetop, A Christmas Story, represents his first foray into fiction.

He calls Gilbert, Arizona home. One wife, five kids, 6 grandkids (and counting), one dog, three books published, and one well-worn laptop.

OTHER WORKS

There's a Message in There Somewhere

"The writings of Brad McBride fill you with a sweet taste of common sense in an often bitter world. Filled with wit, wisdom, life lessons and love, there is something for all to benefit from in this collection."

~*John H. Groberg, beloved author and church leader*

There's a Message OUT There Somewhere

"My favorite way to learn is by stories. I will remember a principle or moral much better if it's taught to me in a story. This is filled with tender and personal stories from one man (and his family) and his moments with the Divine. We all have triumphs, struggles, and failures and we can choose to see God and what He may want us to learn in them if we continually seek Him. Mr. McBride proves this over and over with his talent of story telling."

For more, visit www.ThusWeSee.com

Made in the USA
Monee, IL
28 December 2021